TEMPTATIONS

VOLUME 3

A collection of erotic stories

Edited by Miranda Forbes

Published by Accent Press Ltd – 2009
ISBN 9781907016301

Printed and bound by CPI Group (UK) Ltd, Croydon, CR0 4YY

Cover design by
Red Dot Design

Contents

In Medias Res
by Beverly Langland

"Post nubila Phoebus!" I rolled my eyes. What sort of answer was that? Art is an intellectual snob – a professor of Latin or something equally pretentious at Yale. How Dan and he had ever become friends, I'll never understand. They are like chalk and cheese. Dan, down to earth, had a modest mid-management position with a building firm, while Art looked like he'd never used his hands in his life. "We shared a girl once in college," was Dan's glib reply when I asked. "Art's come to return the favour." Yeah, right! Dan had a huge grin on his face so I assumed he was winding me up. I had recently made the mistake of admitting a recurring fantasy of mine – you know the classic – where I take two cocks at the same time. Luckily, Dan has always been adventurous in bed – and out of it. He indulged my fantasy, pretending someone was with us as he used a dildo on me while I sucked his cock. It created the illusion of another man sharing our bed, but it was just that – a fantasy. In all the years we had been together, Dan had never expressed any desire to share me.

Joke or not, I couldn't get the image of Dan with Art and his girlfriend out of my mind. It certainly changed my opinion of the American. I couldn't picture the stuck-up git getting down and dirty. Nor Dan for that matter. Art's flight had been delayed a day so we were stuck with him overnight. When I asked if he minded he gave his answer in Latin, never offering a translation. He made me feel so ignorant. Art didn't want to go to the pub so we ended up watching a wildlife documentary of all things. I suppose he is into that sort of thing. I sat on the floor by Dan's feet painting my toenails. Art seemed curiously quiet. He usually had something to say about everything and anything. It may have been my imagination or perhaps the image of lions mating but I felt a tingle of expectation in the air. Somehow, certainly without conscious effort on my part the atmosphere in the room had become sexually charged.

I looked up and saw that Art was staring up my skirt. Dan noticed too, but instead of any display of concern or anger, he wormed his foot between my legs and wriggled his toes against my crutch. I snapped my legs shut in surprise, unintentionally trapping his foot. He continued to rub against me so I searched his face questioningly. Dan smiled and nudged my thighs apart. I hadn't imagined it. They were definitely up to no good. It never occurred to me that I had become the focus in some strange game the two of them played. However, I *was* conscious that Dan was showing me off – literally. I was miffed yet aroused at the same time. So aroused I was willing to play the pawn in their bizarre game. Anyway, my panties were already wet. A fact I suspected Art could plainly see. For some reason, that notion alone made me wetter still.

I tried to concentrate on painting the nails on the other foot. I did abysmally. Dan's toes were too distracting. He had found my clitoris and insisted on teasing. I was so excited. From Dan's insistent rubbing. From the fact that I had my legs spread lewdly and Art watched silently. Because my husband apparently *wanted* him to watch! I realised the quiet 'evening in' had been prearranged, but to satisfy my fantasy or Dan's? Did it actually matter? I had never been able to find two men at the same time with whom I felt comfortable enough to engage in a threesome. Dan obviously trusted this man for whatever reason. So, I kept my legs sprawled and let Art look. I lifted my gaze to meet his and held it. The look he gave me was so full of heat that it forced a rush of blood to my pussy, flooding it with moisture. His dark eyes revealed everything he planned to do to me.

"Undo her blouse." Every nerve ending in my body jumped to life. What I had mistaken for arrogance was Art's sense of authority. I understood then. Art is a natural leader, Dan a follower. My hand jumped to the front of my blouse, but I didn't resist as one by one Dan fumbled with the buttons until the material hung free. I don't know why the idea of exposure thrilled me, yet my whole body tingled with anticipation. I reached up and removed my bra, impatient to show this commanding man my breasts. Dan muttered a low, territorial growl in warning. I ignored him. He had forfeited any right of complaint as soon as his foot pushed my thighs open. "Touch your nipples." Without even considering Dan's feelings, I obeyed.

Dan started to insinuate his toes past the side elastic of my panties. I felt the material bunch to one side, felt air on my hot flesh, felt Dan's toe in my wetness. I abandoned all pretence of coyness. I held on to his foot, drew his toes deeper into me. Art slipped from his chair and sat next to me on the floor. In one quick movement, he had undone Dan's fly and had my husband's cock out into the

4

open. I expected Dan to object. He didn't. Art grasped the base of Dan's hardening flesh and began to move his hand up and down. My eyes grew wide. I had mentally prepared myself for the expected threesome, but I had never imagined the two guys would get it on. I stared in fascination as he gently squeezed Dan's balls. Art's eyes bore into mine, challenging me to say something. His lips brushed against my ear, and his teeth softly nibbled my earlobe, sending shivers all down my side. I shuddered as the shockwaves of orgasm ran through me.

I had little respite before Art's hand was in my hair. He drew me down onto Dan's cock, guided it towards my mouth. I bent my head down over him, licked the little dripping mouth, running my tongue-tip round the underside of the head before I swallowed him, lightly dragging my teeth back along his shaft as I withdrew. Dan loves it when I do that. Then I began the process of slowly bobbing my head back down over him, taking him into the back of my mouth, rasping the rough underside with the edge of my bottom teeth. Art's hand pressed down on the back of my head as I descended, but I resisted. The idea of him 'forcing' me onto Dan's cock excited me. Disappointingly, Art didn't respond, instead he let me continue at my own pace. However, he did go behind me to lift my skirt. I was gushing in expectation by then, convinced he was going to fuck me. Sure enough, Art peeled off my soaking panties. I lifted my knees to help him, felt a finger enter me, then another and I pushed back against them. I pushed between Dan's thighs running my tongue up his taut scrotum anticipating the feel of Art's cock. Instead, Art was back at my side, lifting me and edging me forward. I realised he wanted me to straddle Dan. For a second time he took hold of Dan's cock, holding it upright while Dan carefully manoeuvred me onto him like an expensive piece of equipment until he was fully embedded. I could feel Art's fingers squashed between us kneading Dan's balls.

I writhed in pleasure as Art nibbled in the hollow of my neck. Dan let me get used to the feel of him inside me, and then his hands were on my hips encouraging me to move. I slid up and down his pole, Dan pushing up to meet me in time with my strokes. I kissed Dan like we hadn't kissed in a long time. He responded just as enthusiastically. I moaned into his mouth as I thrust downwards to impale myself certain that from his ringside seat Art would be pleased with my enthusiasm. I felt Art shift on the settee. I opened my eyes to find him kneeling beside us. He had stripped naked and his erect cock loomed large in line with my mouth.

I am one of nature's cock worshippers. I poked out my tongue and touched the tip tentatively. It twitched. I looked to Dan for guidance. Would he be angry if I … It seemed he wouldn't since his hands were in my hair pushing me towards it. Obediently I opened my mouth and took Art inside, or at least the part of Art that took my fancy. I tasted immediately the salty pre-come coating the bulbous head. I wasn't going to be able to take all of him into my mouth so I settled for taking his large pink head. I gladly sucked on it greedily, Dan's hands gently resting on the back of my head, his encouragement exciting me even more. I took all I could into me, sliding him to the back of my mouth. Yet, no sooner had I started to relish the feel of his hardness and it was gone.

I opened my eyes to see Art's cock pressed against Dan's lips. I felt a surge of excitement. What would Dan do? I willed him to take it. At college, a close friend had shown me a gay men's magazine. I'll never forget the rush I got looking at two large dicks rubbing up against each other. It turned me on because men turn me on. Hard cocks turn me on. Slowly Dan's lips parted – he was understandably hesitant. But just as I had hoped, excitement finally overtook him and his tongue reached out to lick Art's prick. I watched Dan's face and saw he too was excited. I reached for my nipples, squeezed hard to stop myself from coming as I watched my husband swallow another man's cock. Art withdrew from Dan's mouth and I pounced on the bobbing member eagerly. This time Dan's eyes were serious as I sucked Art deeper. I was conscious of Dan watching. I felt him grow harder deep within my pussy as I momentarily swallowed Art whole. I felt like a whore. I like sucking cock, but to be honest all I could think about at that moment was Dan's willingness to do so. I wanted to watch Art fucking my husband's mouth.

The second time Dan took Art more eagerly. Art pumped in and out of Dan's mouth just the same as if it were mine. I slid up and down on Dan's cock while I watched, mimicking the movement, feasting on the sumptuous vision before me. I brushed the hair away from my face and lowered my lips to Art's balls, licking the underside of them and carefully taking one into my mouth. I gently rolled it around on my tongue, sucking it back and forth at the same time as Dan sucked Art's cock into his mouth. From then on, Dan and I took turns sucking Art until it became too much for the visitor. He abandoned the rotation and simply slid his throbbing cock between the two of us. Dan and I pressed our lips either side of it while Art slid back and forth, clamped between two eager sets of lips. The sensation was bizarre, my face inches from Dan's as we both worshipped this strange man's cock. It is a disgusting thought I know, yet I hoped Art would come on us both. I wanted to kiss Dan, to feel the sticky porridge in his mouth, for him to relish it in mine.

Sadly, Art showed more control. Instead he moved away and encouraged Dan to lie back on the settee. I shuffled with him, disappointed at the lost opportunity, but keen to continue the adventure. I wondered what this imaginative man intended next. He gently pressed against my back until I lay sprawled on top of Dan, face to face, my tits pressed against his chest. Dan kissed me eagerly and I again thought of the missed opportunity. Then I felt hands on my bottom, fingers prising my cheeks apart. My own juices had made me slippery and Art's finger slid easily into my bottom, making my hips buck as waves of pleasure went through me. For a moment, I thought Art was preparing to fuck me back there but as it turned out the intrusion was far more subtle.

"God, he's licking my arse!" I gasped when Dan and I parted for breath. I didn't know what I expected Dan to do about it. As Art curled his tongue and probed deeper I wasn't sure what *I* wanted to do about it. I loved the feel of him slobbering against my anus. The sensation was indescribable. He slowly licked my anus while Dan's cock slid in and out of my cunt. He was driving me wild. *They* were driving me wild! I rode Dan like something possessed and he bucked wildly in response. Art's hands were on my hips, his face buried deep in the crease of my bottom, desperately clinging on for dear life. He probed deeper and deeper, pumping his narrowed rigid tongue-tip in and out in tiny imitation of the movement of Dan's cock. "Now he's fucking my arse with his tongue," I screamed into Dan's mouth.

My frenzied outburst was too much for Dan. I tightened my grip on his cock as he fucked me in earnest, arching up as I pushed down. He rammed into me harder and harder, and I knew it couldn't be long before he would come. Dan was grunting, making animal sounds I'd never heard him make before. Art's hands gripped my hips tighter, and I thrust back against him, wriggling to take even more of his tongue. I didn't know whether to push down onto Dan's cock or push back against Art's tongue. I sighed in ecstasy, totally surrendering to the dual sensation. I fought my rising orgasm, trying to prolong the exquisite pleasure, but the end was inevitable. Then, with a sudden upward lunge, Dan pushed as far into me as he could. I felt his whole body stiffen as he shot his load into me. I came instantly, only vaguely aware that Art was kneeling over me furiously pounding on his cock. I half-turned in time to see him spray his semen onto my quivering bottom. I flopped forward into my husband's waiting arms, pushing my mouth against his, trying to muffle myself as I came again and we all collapsed in a sweaty, exhausted heap.

As their cocks withered and we returned to reality, Dan looked at me with a mixture of embarrassment and apology. I flashed him a loving smile, reassuring him he had nothing for which to apologise, though I suspected that come the cold light of morning Dan would feel differently. As for Art, he was due to catch his flight back to America the next day. I felt a mixture of disappointment and relief. A part of me wanted him to stay so we could explore other scenarios. Fact was I would probably never see him again, which would circumnavigate any awkwardness. For some reason I felt empowered by the whole experience and I realised I had a small window of opportunity on which to capitalise. Carpe diem, I mused. The one phrase of Latin I knew. The only problem I foresaw was deciding to which of these gorgeous men I should surrender my anal virginity. My loving husband or the dark-eyed stranger? I reached out and took a cock in each hand, stroking and kneading them until they were again erect. Oh well … I figured I'd cross that bridge when – and if – we got to it.

No Pan Kissa
by Cyanne

There was a warm breeze in the night air, as spring was taking hold of London and bringing with it a feeling of possibility. It had been a long day and our laughter bordered on hysteria as we walked through Soho towards Madam Jojo's.

As we cut down a side street the garish neon seemed to intensify around a flashing pink sign in Japanese. A new bar had opened by the look of things. Venues came and went all the time, taking the in-crowd with them, but this one seemed to be causing a stir, with stag groups revelling around outside and the old school kerb-crawler types in macs who still haunted the area creeping past like throwbacks from the pre-fashion bona fide red-light district days. Two stunning young Asian girls in race queen outfits were flyering outside the door and beckoning the grinning stags and their entourages into the venue, which, as we walked past, I saw was called No Pan Kissa.

'What do you reckon 'no pan' means?' Charlotte said. 'Is it some crazy new cooking thing without pans. Maybe it's all raw. Maybe they have special …'

'It means no panties.' Jason cut her coke-addled musings short.

'No fucking panties? Is that the customers or the staff?'

We all laughed.

'The staff. It's a Japanese thing. In Kyoto in the 80s and 90s they had these bottomless waitress cafes and all the pervy old businessmen would pay extra for their coffee for an occasional glimpse of pussy. They all got shut down or went out of fashion or something. I'm pretty sure that's what it is though.'

'Seems a bit mental, even for Soho!'

While the other girls tutted and let rip with their inner feminists my pussy got wet at the thought of a hot waitress in a short uniform bending over and flashing her pussy, and even more so imagining that waitress was me. We walked down the street and I craned my neck back towards the little den of iniquity. One of the promo girls did a high kick and I swear she had nothing on under her little yellow skirt. The stag party pushed each other around to get a better look. I was smitten. It was no use trying to get my work mates to go and have a better look, I generally find it's better to hide the fact that I'm a dirty bitch from the people I work with, so I texted my filthiest fuck buddy, JD, and said I had a surprise for him and to meet me tomorrow.

When I got back from the gig I Googled 'No Pan Kissa' and sure enough what Jason said was true. I don't think I've ever rubbed one out to a Wikipedia entry before but I came hard and soaking wet to the unemotive descriptions of the Tokyo trend for cafes where a glimpse of hot young pussy was served up alongside the shabu shabu.

I met JD for a drink first and he filled me in on his latest conquests; a threesome with two performance artists and bedding a fetish model from Poland, I knew I'd picked the right companion to accompany me into the no panties café. As we strolled through Soho JD slipped his hand around my waist and his hand found his way under my skirt and over my thigh, finding it free of even the skimpiest thong.

'Getting into the spirit of things are we?' JD said with an appreciative smile.

'I couldn't help myself', I said, already soaking at the prospect of what we were going to see.

The flyer girls were outside again, wearing

classic porno Japanese schoolgirl uniforms – black pleated skirts, white shirts and socks and striped ties. As we approached they called out 'Irashaimasu!' in their irresistible tones.

Inside was as much a neon nightmare as the exterior. Urgent Japanese pop blasted out of a 1950s jukebox while animé played on huge screens above a brightly lit high-tech coffee bar. Vending machines offered Hello Kitty phone charms and Pokemon toys alongside crotchless panties and flavoured condoms. A sushi conveyor carried elaborate creations around the room, bizarrely high up the wall out of most people's reach.

A stunning waitress with bright blue hair showed us to a table and handed us laminated menus decorated with coquettish girls teasing the hems of their skirts, and brash yellow bubbles offering tea for £10 a pot and sushi for £20 a dish. We ordered tea and lapped up the unbelievable sights. JD slipped his hand under the table and stroked my thigh, just stopping short of my pussy, knowing it would drive me wild as I indulged my inner Sapphic voyeur.

'What do you think that conveyor belt's all about then?' JD asked, sliding his finger between my lips and grazing my clit.

I moaned softly.

'Like I can concentrate on anything while you're doing that!'

Our waitress returned with a tray of green tea in little black bowls. She placed it on our table and tilted the tray, letting a pair of chopsticks fall to the ground.

'Very sorry,' she said. 'Allow me.'

She turned her back to us and bent from the waist to pick them up. Her tiny pleated skirt flipped up exposing her perfect behind and we both gasped as her pussy pouted up at us. She stayed there for a few seconds and I almost came as JD stroked my clit so gently, then she stood up and walked away, leaving us both breathless. We'd been to God knows how many strip clubs but there was something so much naughtier about a waitress 'accidentally' flashing her cunt.

We'd hardly got our breath back when the mystery of the sushi belt was solved when two American businessmen ordered from it. Their tiny waitress beckoned over the huge doorman. He walked over and ran his hands up her legs, under her skirt and lifted her up to the conveyor belt, pulling her skirt up to the waist, right at the eye level of the men. The belt moved slowly and she lifted dishes down one by one, offering small plates of sashimi, shrimp and makizushi while the men's eyes darted from her bare body to the food on offer. When they selected their dishes, the doorman lowered her down and she coquettishly smoothed down her skirt with a practised art of fetish, knowing that a hint of shame makes exposure ten times more exciting.

It was more than I could stand. JD nodded towards the unisex toilets and I followed him in, barely attempting to not look suspicious.

We fell into a cubicle and I grabbed at his flies.

'Not tonight, honey, this is all about you'.

He pressed me back into the wall and ran his hands up my legs.

'Close your eyes.'

His hands ran higher and my skirt lifted.

'The whole café's going to see your pussy. Can you feel how bare you are? How exposed you look?'

He pushed higher and pulled my legs apart slightly.

'All the men are looking at you.'

He buried his face into my pussy and started to lick. I pulled his head into me and melted into the sensation. He knew just how to get me off, circling my clit with his tongue then backing off and pressing light kisses all over my pussy, teasing me into a delicious climax. I pulled my skirt back down shyly, mirroring what I'd seen the waitress do.

'You'll have to walk about with a wet little pussy all night now won't you? Anyway, are you going to make this little fantasy a reality and get a job here or what?'

I was shocked, and aroused, at the thought.

'Oh my God, JD, I couldn't! What if someone from work came in?'

'You only live once honey. Dream it or live it.'

The thought played on my mind as we walked back through the café, watching the girls going about their dirty business. It played on my mind as JD fucked me on the sofa when we got home, when I went to the gym that weekend, and when I sat at my desk on Monday morning beavering away at a PR campaign proposal for a new line of beauty boosting vitamin supplements, in fact I though about little else until I found myself walking in to meet the manager to talk about a job.

The manager was a smart American-Japanese woman in her forties. She openly told me about her days as a waitress at Johnny, the original no pan kissa in Tokyo, and how she thought it was time, in the current climate of extremely graphic porn, to bring back a bit of tease, and a hint of the forbidden. It was doing so well, she said, that she needed new girls all the time, and that I could start that same night. If I'd had time to go away and think about it I'd have more than likely chickened out, but I was delirious with excitement at being one of those fantasy girls.

A French girl in her late twenties, Dionne, was assigned to show me the ropes and she led me into a back room lined with mirrors and stacked with costumes. Clip in hair extensions of all colours and lengths hung on the mirrors, and boxes of MAC makeup and bottles of Issay Miyake perfume sat on the counters, all free to use. Books of Harajuku fashion lay around, as inspiration, she told me, and a TV played cheesy Para Para disco dance videos on a loop. I selected an outfit from a huge rack of clothes, a tiny blue kilt and matching top, with white over the knee socks and platform shoes, and Dionne fashioned my hair into ostentatious pigtails while she talked me through how it all worked.

'You're on commission on top of your basic wage, for any sushi or sake you sell. There's a private room where you can entertain the high rollers, it's just like being a geisha, but without panties! You put on special clothes then and make a lot of money, I'll show you later.'

She winked at me in the mirror, and I barely recognised myself. The PR girl had given way to a porno princess, a waitress pretending to be unaware of her sexual power over the men she serves, except this time that's the name of the game, and everyone's in on it. A perfect post-modernisation of the centuries-old dynamic.

I walked out onto the floor and approached my first table, a group of students, my legs shaking with nerves. Dionne had told me that tea was just a little flash, so when I returned with their bowls from the bar, I curtsied briefly, pulling the folds of my kilt apart at the front. Their eyes glued to my pussy, their faces falling when I let go and covered myself with the tiny skirt. I was hooked, and so horny I had to nip into the toilets and play with myself.

I flaunted myself shamelessly, enjoying every second of it, lapping up the adoration without any fear of reprisal from the men about being teased, or from other women about acting slutty. I had full permission and, crazily, was getting paid handsomely for the privilege.

Around midnight Dionne came over to me and said some regular customers, big spenders, had come in and wanted a back room party with two hostesses.

'I'll tell you all about it while we change. Come on, it's great fun and you can earn a packet in tips. You're sexy, I want to do a party with you'.

We went into the back room and she handed me a hanger with a tiny red skirt made of flippy, flimsy fabric, and a matching bikini top.

'We wear these for the first drink and food, then we change for the dessert and drinks. The guys sit around and we serve them three courses, plus sake and tea, and chat with them. They pay a fortune for it and we get £500 each. If they tip you, give them a little flash. Sometimes they like to pull your skirt up themselves, they should give you £100 for it, and always act a bit embarrassed, like you didn't realise he was going to do it. Also there are fans in the floor and they have buttons they can press which make your skirt blow up. It's best to pretend like it's a shock and you're shy about having no panties on though. I know you're not though. You love it.'

I stammered something but she just smiled at me. Looks like I wasn't the only one not doing it for the money.

She led me to the bar where we collected trays of sake-bombs, tall pint glasses of beer with chopsticks balanced on the top holding a shot glass of sake. Dionne led the way into the private room, which was a more understated and traditional Japanese dining room with a low table and bamboo screen.

Eight suited men were sat around on cushions and I quickly realised that, as well as a nod to tradition, this was also a device for the best view of our cunts as we walked around serving, and I wasn't complaining one little bit. The men, obviously very rich and powerful, were transfixed by trying to glimpse my pussy as I moved carefully around, struggling a little with the bondage of the tall drinks and the high heels.

One of the men pressed a button on the table and a huge gust of wind blew up from the floor, effortlessly throwing the tiny skirt way above my waist. I squirmed with pleasure as the men made approving noises and made a theatrical attempt to cover myself, and acted flustered when the gust died down and my skirt returned to offering a hint of modesty. Dionne smiled at me.

We served hand-prepared sushi while the men peeped up our skirts and pressed the fans, and after the main course one of them handed me two fifty pound notes. I smiled shyly, wondering if he would ever imagine that I was enjoying this as much as he was, and he grasped the front of my skirt and yanked it up, exposing my cunt clearly to the room. The men gasped and I writhed, pretending to try to get away, feeling like throwing myself into their collective arms to be ravished.

Dionne and I cleared the dishes and she led me back into the changing rooms.

'We change now for the final courses', she said, handing me a see through plastic apron trimmed with white PVC and a tiny pink bra. As she changed into hers my heart leapt as I realised there were no bottoms, just the transparent aprons which had little coverage at the front and none at all from the back! My pussy looked so rude through a window of clear PVC and my nipples were peaking out of the top of the tiny bra. We walked to the now crowded bar to collect trays of sweets, fruit and sorbet and all eyes were on us and our pussies. Dionne walked ahead of me and I felt a surge of lust for a woman so confident that she can walk through a crowded room wearing just a few scraps of transparent PVC and flimsy lace.

The men cheered as we entered the room with the desserts, and money began flying in our direction. Dionne pulled me up onto the table with her and I followed her lead as she picked up sweets and hand fed them to the men, always bending over slowly and deeply, showing off her gorgeous cunt to the men behind her. Piles of money were amassing at our feet. I bent over the let one of the men lick a glob of lemon sorbet off my finger and felt an icy slither down my back. I turned sharply and Dionne was grinning at me, her hand full of ice cream. I wasted no time and picked up a handful of strawberries, mashed them in my hand and smeared them on her tits, pulling them out of her bra as I did. The men went wild, throwing more money and banging on the table.

Dionne picked up a huge bowl of sorbet and I wrestled her for it, falling to our knees. She grabbed a handful of it and pushed it in my face, then leaned in to lick it off and we were kissing lasciviously. Her hands were all over me and she pushed me back onto the table and licked the sorbet and fruit off my tummy and pulled my little apron to one side. Dionne lapped at my pussy and slid a finger gently inside me and I cried out with pleasure. I opened my eyes and all the men were staring in awe as her gorgeous dark hair settled on my thighs, stuck with sticky fruit and sorbet, our bodies moving together, my hands curled in her hair. Her tongue wriggled relentlessly and I came hard, thrashing around in the wrecked desserts, the men clapping and cheering.

One night working at No Pan Kissa was enough for me, I fulfilled the fantasy, there was no need to push my luck and get caught by my increasingly curious work colleagues who were laughing and joking about the place while I kept my head down, prim in my office clothes pretending to be engrossed in the latest book release or exhibition opening.

I kept in touch with Dionne though. Very close touch in fact. One day we might even treat JD to a dinner party. I never did thank him properly for encouraging me to live out my fantasy.

Room Service
by Alcamia

'Darling, you really must loosen up.' Henrietta urged. 'You're far too sexually tight. Let me take you on a nice little shopping trip to New York and we'll stay at the Hotel Delice. In no time at all, you'll feel like a new woman.'

I loved Henrietta because she was so unconventional. She smoked offensive strong black cigarillos and drank tequila like a man, besides which she had an unquenchable and unorthodox appetite for sex.

Henrietta always stayed at the Hotel Delice since she said it offered unique room service. As I stepped inside I was struck by the hotel's curious ambiance and its air of studied decadence. My room itself, was stylish with heavy flocked wallpaper and period deco furniture. Henrietta assured me the Delice was once the haunt of movie starlets and politicians. I could certainly imagine Marlene Dietrich stereotypes swooning and fucking on the furniture.

'You're right, it has a certain dilapidated charm and a fabulous vibe.' Draping my coat over a chair, I pushed open the bathroom door. The bathroom was luxurious with gold taps and an extensive provision of fragrant soaps and oils.

'I knew you'd like it.' Henrietta enthused. 'But it has more charms than you may at first think. This hotel has quite a reputation and it has some very special members of staff. Staff, who go out of their way to make you feel good. But one thing darling. You mustn't be shocked or scandalised by what transpires here and more importantly, you mustn't complain to management.'

'Whatever are you on about?' I laughed. 'Why would I want to complain?'

'Well Carla. One of the specialities of this hotel is its unique brand of room service which has been delighting women of a certain age, for decades. A woman must always avail herself of room service at the Hotel Delice, it's the hotel's one truly unforgettable experience.'

'Is this one of your jokes Henrietta?'

She winked suggestively. 'Definitely not. I just want you to share in my delightful little find. Just never on any account, spill the beans.' She clapped her hand to her mouth. 'Perhaps I shouldn't have said anything at all.'

Henrietta was insufferable. I had given up trying to analyse her ages ago. She had a flair for the dramatic and an extremely crude and filthy imagination.

When she left me, I sat in a chair for a moment. I really ought to have ordered some soothing champagne to relax me, as I could never sleep in a strange bed. Champagne was my one small concession in life.

So, I dialled room service.

When I opened the door, room service stepped inside. He was the most amazing man I had ever encountered, exuding such a potent sexual charisma he made my skin tingle. I stared mesmerised, into his acutely golden eyes which were already mentally undressing me. 'You ordered champagne madam. Shall I uncork and pour?'

'That would be nice?' I watched him with interest as he opened the bottle with only the merest hint of a pop. 'If you don't mind me making an observation madam. You have exquisite hair. It reminds me of the colours of autumn, and your eyes are so intensely green.'

It was rather impertinent of room service to make such personal remarks but the flattery made me feel instantly warm. 'Oh!' I stretched up self-consciously, to touch my riot of red curls. 'My brother calls my hair an explosion in a fireworks factory.'

His eyes roamed impudently over my face. 'I can imagine if someone carefully lit your fuse, you'd explode very well yourself.'

I experienced a sharp intake of breath. 'Goodness you're daring for room service. Do you speak to all your clients like this?'

He shrugged. 'Not all of them!'

I sipped the champagne. He was flirting with me.

'You look rather tense.' Stepping forward room service stroked a tendril of hair away from my cheek and then dug his fingers into the tight muscles around my shoulders.

'Oh do I? How astute of you.' I forced a watery smile. 'I'm still a bit spun out from the flight. You see, I hate flying. However it's an unnecessary evil in this day and age.'

'You need to relax. You're like a bundle of knotty string.'

'And you're rather cheeky.'

Room service shrugged. 'I just say it, like it is. You're also beautiful, that hair's a potent aphrodisiac for me. I bet your snatch is the same fiery red?'

'I ought to slap you. You're so rude.'

'All you have to do is say the word and I'll

leave. But I don't think you really want me to.' He raised an eyebrow

'No don't go yet.' I heard myself say. 'I'm curious. My friend tells me, the room service here, is second to none.'

'Oh it is. I'm at your service and I aim to provide an unforgettable experience.'

'Henrietta made the staff at this hotel sound so fabulously mysterious.'

'There's nothing mysterious about me, I can assure you. I'm just the straightforward room service boy.'

'You seem very cultured.' I insisted. 'Couldn't you find something better to do?'

'Why find something better? This is the perfect job for me. I adore it and I'm an expert at it. I meet many fascinating women and I enjoy flattering them, making them feel good.'

'If I didn't know better, I'd say you were an undercover gigolo.'

He laughed, shaking his head. 'Oh I'm neither of those.'

One shirt button was open, exposing a smooth tanned chest. I couldn't remember seeing that open button before. I was sexually attracted to him; it was hard not to be. He had that tousled easiness about him which was so appealing to my senses. He was the kind of man who would enjoy the outdoors. Yachting, horse back riding. He was a wild, untamed creature squeezed into a suit. Now that was fascinating. And he could easily draw you out. He reminded me of a good journalist I'd once met. I'd said I would not talk, yet before I knew it he had mesmerised me and the words tumbled. It is a gift to be able to do that and not many people have it. I felt a surge of eroticism race through me, a sexual torrent which moistened my sex.

'I shouldn't be keeping you talking room service, you must be busy.'

'On the contrary.' He poured me more champagne. 'Drink up. The champagne makes your eyes sparkle.'

I sat down and unbuckling my shoes I began to massage my feet. 'Here let me do that.' Before I could stop him, he was kneeling with my feet on his lap and he was kneading them. The kneading felt very good. He was a magician in the use of thumb and finger. Instantly the rhythmical motions relaxed me and the tension ebbed from my shoulders and back. 'I could run you a bath. You look tired?'

'You have to be kidding.'

'Not at all. I offer a unique and personal service. I'll pull the drapes, turn down the bed and draw your bath. Whatever you wish? And the best part is. There's no charge and I don't accept tips or gratuities.

'There must be a reward of some kind?'

'Yes, yes there is.' His eyes glittered. 'I have the satisfaction of making a beautiful woman happy.'

I should have told him to leave but I could not. If you had met him yourself, you would know what I mean. I did not ask him to leave the room, because it seemed right that he was there. I later discovered all women felt the same about room service and that is why he had kept his job at the Delice for so many years. He was very special, and he had the unique gift of being able to extract the sex out of women. You could immediately fall in love with him and I could imagine him on my arm as the perfect companion. Flirtatious, gracious and indulgent, he made you feel as if you possessed a power over him, like you had some ingredient he desired. I could not for the life of me think what that ingredient was, but it made me feel as if I were the most desirable woman on the planet.

He strolled into the bathroom.

I watched him through the crack in the door, as he stirred the water with his hand, tested it for heat with his elbow, and added generous splashes of expensive oil, before laying out the fluffy white towels. 'What's your name?' He said when he returned. 'I cannot forever be thinking of you as

Madame X.'

'My name's Carla and what's yours?'

'Just call me RS. Do you have a bath robe or a nightdress, Carla?'

I motioned towards the wardrobe. 'Yes, inside there. I never wear a nightdress. I sleep nude.' I studied his face to see if I had elicited a reaction, but his expression remained implacable. I was fascinated, wondering where all this sexual flirtatiousness would lead.

He brought me the robe and then he helped me to my feet. 'Thank you.' I said unsteadily.

'You must have jet lag. I expect you're tired?'

'Yes very. I shall be going straight to bed after my bath, but I doubt I'll sleep.'

'I'll make you a sandwich. I'll go down to the kitchen this instant. 'What would you like? Let me guess. Caviar, salmon?' RS grinned.

'You really are extraordinary. However there's no need.'

'There's a great need.' He replied, smiling at me as he clicked the door shut.

I sank into the bath water, allowing the warm comforting ocean to engulf me and soon I was drifting in a satisfyingly serene vacuum. I heard the door open and when I opened my eyes, RS was sitting on the side of the bath tub. 'I brought your sandwich it's in the other room. Do you want me to soap your back now?'

'Do you always follow women into their bathrooms? Are you a pervert? Is this how you get your kicks?'

'Of course not. I just enjoy providing an enhanced service.'

'I see.' I handed him the soap. I was enjoying the thought of his hands on my naked flesh. I closed my eyes as RS's fingers explored my wet skin. He had wonderfully sensual hands, which followed each line and contour of my nakedness as if he were fashioning me out of clay. He kneaded the tenseness out of my neck with his knuckles and then he washed my hair, massaging my scalp with delicious circular movements. I awakened, my skin tingling with a million sensations, my nipples firming and my sex softening. He lathered his hands and impudently caressed my breast and I allowed him to. Then, taking a little of the soap on his finger he palpated and circled the swollen globe, moving closer and closer to my erect nipple, before pinching it between thumb and forefinger. I wanted to orgasm as the arousal from his touch ignited my sex, but I felt inhibited.

'I'm ready to get out of the bath now.' I stood up and he cloaked me in the towel, helping me out of the deep bath. I stumbled on the wet tiles, falling against him and he caught me and pulled me gently into his hips. Then, he gently rubbed my wet breasts and my back and dried the cleft between my buttocks, assiduously sliding the towel between the folds of my sex wet pussy. Finally he held up the robe.

'I don't need that.' I said shortly, as in my curiosity I forgot my inhibition and began to wonder how far I could tease him and what the resolution to such protracted foreplay would be. Indeed I had forgotten everything now except how much I desired seduction. I decided I would like to drop the towel, and I did so. I caught a glimpse of myself in the full length wardrobe mirror, and I admit I looked splendid for a woman of a certain age. I was voluptuous, and when I unpinned my hair, it fell in a cascade around my shoulders. I posed, thrusting out my hips, I was being daring.

RS's eyes were glistening with subdued hunger. He drew out a chair and shaking out a napkin and spreading it out on my lap he allowed his naughty fingers to graze my naked cunt.

'Why don't you join me? Sit down and have a spoonful of caviar. I won't take no, for an answer.' I flirted. 'But first of all, why don't you unbutton your shirt. Better still take it off. Would you mind doing that?'

RS loosened his tie and as he unfastened the remaining buttons of his shirt, his hair fell rakishly forward over his eyes.

'No! Certainly not Carla. I'm at your service.'
He put mild emphasis on the word service before
sitting down opposite me, buttering toast, adding
caviar and feeding it to me. I opened my mouth
and I obliged him by licking my lips and showing
him my tongue. He wiped a dribble of butter from
my chin as he studied my lips, open and inviting.
The sex rippled off him in cascades of energy.

I wondered if it might be fun to provoke room
service. 'Oh dear, I think I just dropped my
earring. It fell on the floor, and I can't see it.'

Now he was on his hands and knees beneath
the table. I was becoming increasingly daring and
very naughty. I spread my legs, displaying my
cunt. I knew he was looking at me since I could
feel his warm breath disturbing my pubic hair. He
was very close indeed and I shivered with delight.
I then said. 'Lick me.'

I continued to nibble the caviar as I felt his
hands spread my legs further apart. He kissed my
inner thighs and my sex all over, working his way
towards my juicy slit with slow sensuous strokes
and kisses until finally his finger and thumb parted
the lips, and the mouth and tongue began to slide
up and down my cleft, his teeth eventually
fastening on my clitoris. I bit down hard on the
toast as I muffled my moan. RS was now working

his tongue around and around my sex, and I could feel my orgasm beginning to surge. I had to hold the arms of the chair when I came, it was so violent. So totally unexpected.'

He sat back down and he ran a hand through his tousled hair.

'I think I'd like to go to bed now.' I stood up abruptly. 'Would you be so kind as to brush my hair?'

'I'd love to brush your hair. What a pleasure.'

I sat on the bed, my legs wet with cunt juice and the aroma of warm heady sexual arousal emanating from me in sweet waves. RS sat beside me and I admired his firm musculature and the jutting ferocity of his cock pressing against his pants. He teased my hair, easing out the knots and I felt the excitement begin to rise again with each successive tug. I took my breast in my hand and as he brushed my hair, I massaged the nipple until it was firm and sensitive, then I caressed it, inciting my passion, forcing my orgasm. I had never experienced such pleasure, it kept ebbing and receding in deeper and more satisfying pulses. Finally he finished brushing my hair and he lifted it back from my shoulders. I placed my hand gently on his cock.

'Service me.' I commanded flirtatiously as I gazed into his eyes. 'That's what room service is all about, isn't it? That's the purpose of the game?'

He stood in front of me, and unzipping his pants out sprung his liberated penis. Whilst he let me fondle him, he carefully controlled his lust. He was the perfect slave.

I stroked the organ, admiring the plump girth and rippling sinuous length as I stroked the male essence from the bleeding stem. Gently I rubbed up and down the shaft, and sinking to my knees I took the pole between my teeth and I sucked it, as I fondled my clit. Room service stroked my hair and I felt the tensile promise of his climax. He did not move until I was satisfied.

My fantasy had always been to discover men and peel away the layers of them to reach the heart of their arousal, however usually men were too eager to be inside me. RS allowed me to explore all of him at my leisure. I slipped my finger into the tight constriction of his butt and he sighed as I drew him to the brink of ejaculation and then away again.

We played endless games of pleasure as I acted out my fantasies. I dribbled champagne between my thighs and he sucked each droplet away as I made him clean me with his tongue. Then I lowered myself onto him, spearing his cock inside me, on my terms. I wanted to cry out with the passion of it, the controlled thrusting deliciousness of it. He was the perfect lover, timing his orgasm to perfection as the penis rotated and thrust inside me. Using tongue and cock to take me to the very boundaries of ecstasy he wrapped me in the sheet and stroked my hair.

I awoke at three thirty am. and I really fancied hot milk. I was smiling coyly as I pressed the button on the phone.

'Oh! Could I order some hot milk please?' Room service had told me he was always available to oblige no matter what the time of day or night.

When he knocked on the door I said to him. 'Don't you get fed up with these calls at all hours?'

Grinning, RS reached once more, to unbutton his shirt. 'Why Carla, I never tire of providing room service.'

The Travelling Circus.
by J.S. Black

I watched with interest the colourful procession of caravans clatter out from the surrounding woodland and into our small village square. 'Madame Juliet's Travelling Circus' had arrived.

I had been sent to fetch milk, but my chore for the moment forgotten I stood amongst my fellow villagers to watch the caravans move slowly through the village, heading for a clearing in the woods which for a short time would be their home.

I suspect that many of the villagers here are wary of our visitors, being so doubtful of anything disrupting their mundane lives, but not I. Being a young woman of eighteen I welcomed any break from the dull routine of village life!

"Ladies and gentlemen!" I looked towards the woman who addressed us from the lead caravan, "roll up and see the show tomorrow night in the clearing just over yonder!" I knew this to be Madame Juliet, her commanding yet deeply feminine tone easily captivating the gathering. And as dwarfs gambolled and lions roared this beautiful woman teased and lured us.

I felt spellbound by her striking blue eyes framed by a mane of long curls the colour of burgundy wine, bought alive under the summer sun, yes, Madame Juliet was indeed a beautiful woman. I think the village men were transfixed by her, and secretly, so was I.

When my eyes fell upon the man whose caravan announced, 'Gabriel the Extraordinaire!' my breath momentarily caught in my throat.

Long dark locks fell about muscular shoulders that strained against the material of his flamboyant shirt but it was Gabriel's eyes that I found most striking. There was something of innocence there, and something else that I could not read, as though he were distant from his surroundings and we held little interest to him at all.

Milk pails forgotten, I pushed my way to the front of the crowd where nobody would be able to block my view of this man that I'd yet to take my eyes from and maybe, I hoped, <u>he</u> might glance my way and notice <u>me</u>.

And notice me he did. If only for a moment his dark and beautiful eyes had met my own and I could only hope that no one but Gabriel had seen the lustful longing that was surely in my own eyes.

"These travelling folk are nothing but trouble. I don't want you anywhere near them, do I make myself clear Anna?" father told me from over the rim of his pipe.

"But father, I'm not a little girl anymore, and so little happens here in this village…" I implored, looking towards my mother for help.

"I'm sorry Anna but your father is right, I'm not keen on those gypsy people, they're not like us, they have strange ways," my mother warned.

The thought of not seeing these people again upset me, I didn't care if they were considered strange. I felt drawn to the travellers and needed so much to see the goddess like Madame Juliet once again and of course, Gabriel…

Being a warm night I tossed back my bed sheets to lie with the moonlight upon me. Slowly, I began to raise my nightgown to expose my young plump thighs, while imagining Gabriel watching me as I did so.

I knew so very little about sex and had virtually no experience apart from when Tommy the ironsmiths son once showed me his cock, and how he rubbed it to make it hard and I'm sure he would've shown me again if my father hadn't caught us. My father had lectured me for hours about the evils of sex and of how we should not give in to temptation.

But there are times, such as now, when I ache between my thighs, when I want so much to explore and to touch myself, such is my frustration!

I know that what I'm doing is wrong, teasing myself as I run my palm over the smoothness of my right leg, moving slowly over my inner thigh… I stop before I touch where my wetness has moistened my panties. I must try to not give into myself but oh, is it so wrong for me to pleasure myself in this way?

I imagine Gabriel, watching me, those powerful yet strangely innocent eyes meeting my own, seeing my desire for naughtiness and it feels delicious when I hook my fingers around the gusset of my panties, to slowly pull the damp material aside and to expose myself to him. With my other hand, my right hand, I resist no longer and touch myself where it pleasures me most, encouraged by Gabriel's gentle smile.

"I'm yours to do with as you so wish sir," I tell my imaginary Gabriel and slowly push two of my fingers deeply into my young tightness, stifling my groan of pleasure before it could escape my mouth.

I thought again about Gabriel and the other travellers so very near. On this balmy summer night a short and pleasant walk would have me at their camp in very little time, and once there, maybe there would be a chance of seeing Gabriel and maybe, secretly hidden by the night, I could watch him for a little while…

With some reluctance I removed my fingers from deep within my thighs and admired how they glistened in the moonlight. I felt the desire to place my fingers to my mouth, to taste myself but I dare not. What was it that hindered my pleasure so? Guilt? Yes, guilt surely. Why did I so crave that which most folk would call sinful?

I looked towards my open window. I saw Gabriel's smile once again, willing me onwards…

The warm soft breeze felt wonderful upon my skin as, wearing only my nightgown, I made my way through the woodland. I wondered if I were being foolish, that I'd reach the caravans only to find them closed and able to see no one, but I'd no intention of turning back now.

Before long I could see the caravans through the clearing trees, their paint shining under the moonlight. The night air carried the sound of voices from the camp along with the sound of what I thought to be a lion murmuring to the night and with effort I crept steadily in my attempt to make no sounds of my own.

A nervous wave washed through me when I saw the warm, welcoming glow from the nearest caravan, Gabriel's caravan, almost touching the edge of the woodland. It had been my intention to remain hidden within the thickets but realizing that from here I would see very little I ventured forwards, out of the cover of darkness and into the silver moonlight.

Lust and excitement pushed aside my feelings of nervousness when on peering through the caravans' small window I saw Gabriel who appeared to be seated, and carefully, I positioned myself so that I might see more.

Gabriel wore only his black leggings and silently, I admired his exposed muscular torso and drank in the sight of his thick dark hair. The sight of him caused a longing in me that was almost painful.

But why was Gabriel tied to the chair, his hands behind his back?

Instinctively, my hand moved under my thin gown, between my thighs…

"I own you, body and soul… slave of mine…" I barely suppressed a surprised yelp on hearing Madame Juliet's deep and commanding voice from within the caravan. My mouth fell open. I needed to see more.

The gypsy woman was relaxing upon a narrow bed on the other side of the caravan where she had raised her gowns to expose her large, dark skinned thighs and her sex between. She wetted her fingers before placing them between her thighs where she made small circular movements. I was fascinated! So I wasn't alone in my desire to pleasure myself in this way! I slowed my own movements upon myself, aware of my closeness to that most wonderful of sensations…

Madame Juliet watched Gabriel intently and when she spoke her movements upon herself quickened, "You like to see me do this to myself don't you Gabriel, can you see how wet I've become…" I watched Madame Juliet place her glistening fingers to her mouth as she watched Gabriel, sucking them before returning them to her most private area. She had performed with such ease and relish that which I myself had been too timid to do… but not after this night…

I returned my gaze to Gabriel. His chest rose deeply with each breath and I noticed a sheen of sweat upon his smooth skin. Although still wearing the leggings, I could see that he was erect under the thin black material.

"I see you straining for release lover, but I may not give it to you yet," Madame Juliet said teasingly and I returned my gaze to her, "I think I might choose to drink your cum tonight… if I so please…" I'd quickened my movements between my thighs and was now unable to stop the wave of pleasure exploding from between my thighs, weakening my knees.

To my horror I'd let out a deep groan of pleasure and quickly, I turned away from the caravan so that I might return to the cover of the night.

I thought I'd run into a tree before feeling powerful hands take hold of my shoulders and looking up, I saw the face of the circus's strongman peering down at me.

"Bring her inside Jareth," I heard Madame Juliet command before being carried towards the opening door of Gabriel's caravan.

"Thank you Jareth, you may go," Madame Juliet ordered and Jareth did as he was told. Inside the caravan I felt overwhelmed. Strange yet pleasant incense enveloped my senses, making me feel pleasantly warm and giddy. I felt afraid and yet excited.

Madame Juliet stood silently for a moment, observing me.

"Are the folk in this village in the habit of watching people then?" she asked, her powerful voice intimidating me.

"No miss," I answered quietly.

"Then why did you come here? Answer me girl," the gypsy woman demanded. I glanced towards Gabriel before lowering my gaze to the floor.

"Please don't tell my father! I'll never say anything I promise!" I suddenly begged.

"Of course you'll say nothing! We're not the ones looking through folks windows are we!" She placed her hand under my chin, lifting my face. "What's your name girl?"

"Anna Marlton," I answered.

"So, <u>Anne Marlton</u>," Madame Juliet's tone softened, "you were innocently walking by and couldn't help your interest in us so had to get a little closer, this right girl?"

"Yes," I answered in eager agreement, "that's just how it was."

"No one innocently walks through woodland at night to peer into windows girl, you'll have to do better than that," she smiled, it seemed that she was amused by me at least. She noticed my gaze towards Gabriel and I guess she read much from my eyes, "Ah, I should have known," the gypsy woman smiled at me. She reached for a bottle placed upon a small table and pouring the liquid into a goblet, handed me the drink. I drank deeply. It was a strong wine the likes of which I'd never tried before and I liked it, it both warmed and soothed me.

Madame Juliet frightened me a little, but I liked her nevertheless.

"Were you touching yourself while watching

us Anna?" Madame Juliet asked with a nod towards the window. The question sounded natural and not meant to embarrass or belittle me. I nodded slowly, my eyes now meeting hers. The gypsy woman nodded with a smile, as if she already knew.

"And this strict father of yours, you have to hide the fact that you're now a young woman whose interest in sex is awakened?"

"How did you know that he's strict?" I asked, feeling that this woman could read me too easily.

"Well, your first response once we caught you here was to beg us not to tell your father," she smiled again, "fathers worry about daughters, it's only natural, and sex is natural too Anna. So, did it feel good to masturbate while watching us?"

I took another sip from my drink, "Yes, but I was also afraid because I knew I was doing wrong, and that I might get caught…"

"Ah, and caught you were!" Madame Juliet laughed not unpleasantly. Gabriel remained silent as he watched me, his eyes giving away little of his thoughts. "But it's not our intention to cause you harm girl," Madame Juliet continued, "indeed you are of interest to us. Tell me exactly what you were doing before you decided to come here."

"I was in my room when I'd begun… I like to imagine things… I wanted to imagine Gabriel watching me…"

"Yes, go on,"

"And I wanted to see him again because I knew you'd all be gone soon, I wanted to fill my thoughts with him so that I could… well…" I struggled to find the words but it seemed that Madame Juliet already knew them,

"Think of him with more clarity for the next time."

"Yes," I answered. I thought I might feel ashamed but I did not. If anything, I'd the desire to place my hand between my thighs once again… with both Madame Juliet and Gabriel as watchers.

"Anna, untie Gabriel." Madame Juliet nodded to where Gabriel was still tied to the chair and feeling sorry that I'd spoilt their fun, I was eager to obey.

Gabriel kept eye contact with me as I neared him, the power behind those eyes, along with his pleasant, exotic aroma, weakening my legs and feeling as if I were approaching one of the circus's cages beasts, I crouched behind his chair to begin unfastening the bindings around his thick wrists. Gabriel was now free.

"Gabriel, tie the girl to the chair," the woman ordered and before I could protest Gabriel had taken hold of my shoulders and lowered <u>me</u> to the chair. He moved quickly, tying my arms behind my back at the wrists. I was at the mercy of the travellers and I suppose I had been from the moment I'd first seen them enter the village.

"You have little experience of what a man and woman can do Anna, but your desire for knowledge has bought you to us," Madame Juliet said. To my surprise she planted a kiss upon my lips before standing away from me once again.

Gabriel stood silently over me, watching me. He smiled gently and I smiled nervously in return.

"You have nothing to fear Anna and you need not worry, no one is going to know what happens out here," the gypsy woman added darkly as she closed the shutters across the small window.

"I've been taught that sex is a nasty thing…" I mumbled, feeling both fear and excitement once again.

"Well, maybe we can teach you otherwise," Madame Juliet said and hooking her thumbs around the hips of Gabriel's leggings, slowly pulled them down. Gabriel's cock sprang upwards now that it was released from the restraining material. It pointed towards me, so close that I noticed how its very tip glistened and feeling a powerful wave of lust wash over me I pulled instinctively at my bindings.

"What's so nasty about this Anna?" Madame Juliet asked. She took Gabriel's cock in her hand

and slowly moved it up and down, close towards the tip where it appeared to swell further.

"Nothing…" I breathed, my bindings frustrating me now. I needed desperately to touch myself and knew that if I were free, I could never have the courage to actually touch Gabriel, who, still held by his cock, was led by the gypsy woman towards the bed where she pushed him down upon it.

"I want you to watch us Anna so that you may think of us in your most private of moments," Madame Juliet told me. She lay upon the bed besides Gabriel, her face positioned close to his cock. Slowly, she closed her mouth around his member to begin sucking noisily and deeply upon it.

"Oh…," I said, my voice little more than a whisper. Gabriel's eyes met mine before he returned his attention to Madame Juliet, his large hand gently stroking the gypsy woman's lush hair. I so desperately needed release and yet could do nothing but watch, unable to believe what I was witnessing.

Madame Juliet pulled her mouth from Gabriel's cock with an audible 'pop,' "Girl, understand that this man would do anything to please me and I him, our pleasure brings us together fully." Changing her position upon the bed, the gypsy woman pulled her gowns up around her waist and I found myself fascinated by her mature, heavy thighs and I longed to run my hand over the length of one of those powerful thighs, to feel the smoothness of her skin. Throwing back her hair, Madame Juliet positioned herself upon Gabriel's cock as he lay upon the bed before slowly lowering herself, drawing in a breath of pleasure as she did so.

I struggled uselessly against my bindings. I needed to pleasure myself and didn't care if they should have seen me… I _wanted_ them to see me!

Madame Juliet ground herself against Gabriel, her eyes closed in concentration as she worked her powerful thighs against his groin. Her quickening breaths became long crying gasps as she reached that wonderful sensation that I knew well enough from my own solitary experiences.

"I… must come… soon…" Gabriel spoke as though he feared disappointing her. Madame Juliet slowed her movements upon Gabriel. She turned her face towards me and I wished then that I could kiss her softened features.

"Would you like to enjoy Gabriel too, Anna?" Madame Juliet asked, "I will be here with you, to guide you."

"Yes, I'll try," my voice betrayed my yearning but I didn't care. I began to feel nervous once again but it served only to fuel my desire.

Gabriel released my bindings quickly and I found myself lifted as though my weight were nothing, to be carried towards the bed where Madame Juliet awaited, a smile upon her face.

As soon as I had been laid upon the bed they were upon me, planting my young body with hungry kisses and I was soon writhing with sheer pleasure from their attention. I tried in desperation to conceal my cries as in turn they tasted deeply my young, very moist cunny. I watched Madame Juliet use her tongue upon me, flicking over my opening before tasting me so deeply that I thought her intention was to fill me with her tongue while Gabriel kissed my face and stroked my long hair. I felt that I would explode, never before had I experienced such intense pleasure.

"Would you like Gabriel to pleasure you now?" Madame Juliet asked, her seductive voice something that I could never imagine refusing. Her face was close to mine now, and when she kissed me, her tongue entering my mouth I could taste my own juices upon her mouth and tongue.

"Be careful with me… please," I begged.

"He will be," she told me.

Gabriel positioned himself between my thighs, his innocent young face watching me as he slowly began to push himself into me, filling me. I knew that I need only to say stop and he would, but I didn't want him to stop, I wanted this.

Madame Juliet planted soft kisses upon my stomach as she moved down the bed to watch closely Gabriel's motions between my thighs. When I let out a cry, it was not one of pain.

"You want him to stop?" the gypsy woman asked gently.

"No, please, I want him to go on; I want him to treat me as he would you," I pleaded. I saw that smile once again upon Gabriel's face as his thrusts became harder, his length filling me and his body pounding against the area where I loved to stroke myself. Madame Juliet planted kisses upon my face. Her tongue traced a line down my neck until her mouth was upon my young breasts where she sucked and kissed before flicking a swollen nipple with her expert tongue. I writhed, totally at their mercy as the height of my pleasure powered through me. So wet was I that I felt my copious juices run from my cunny, down between my bottom to soak the sheet beneath me.

Gabriel groaned into my mouth as he kissed me and I knew what he was soon to do.

"Don't come inside her," Madame Juliet warned when Gabriel's thrusts became more urgent. Part of me wanted him so very much to do so and could only imagine how it might feel.

When, with a grunt, Gabriel withdrew from me, I longed for him to be back there.

I watched, fascinated, as Gabriel held his cock tightly in his huge fist. The force of his first jetting release was such that his thick cum reached my neck and chin and consequent emissions landed in creamy trails over my young pert breasts and stomach in warm streams. Madam Juliet licked and sucked at Gabriel's cum and smiling, returned her mouth to mine...

Both gently wiped me down with warm damp cloths, an act which made me hungry for yet more of their attention. But there was to be no more it seemed.

Madame Juliet bought me a sweet hot drink and ordering me to drink I found it was chocolate.

"You're going to make me leave now aren't you, I don't want to leave," I said glumly, looking from Gabriel to Madame Juliet.

"You must, this is not your home and we don't wish for unwanted attention from your father or any of the villagers," the woman told me not unkindly. I said nothing. I suppose I was sulking.

"Gabriel," Madam Juliet said, "walk Anna back through the woods, make sure she reaches her home safely," the woman ordered and Gabriel, indicating for me to head for the door stood aside to await me.

Gabriel was a man of few words but I was more than happy just to be walking with him through the woodland. We were out of the woodland with my home in view when he spoke, his voice soft,

"We wanted to give you something," Gabriel reached inside of his jacket to produce a package wrapped with cloth. Feeling surprised I took the offered object, thanking him as I did so.

"We really liked you, what we did tonight isn't something we'd do with anybody, but my wife saw something in you that she liked, and I did too," Gabriel said with a smile.

"Your... wife?" I asked.

"Yes, we have been in wedlock for almost ten years, I love her very much," Gabriel said, "now, you must be on your way Anna, please always remember us as we will you," Gabriel leaned forwards and gave me a kiss on the nose. I saw his smile in the moonlight. Without another word he turned and began making his way back through the woods.

"Thank you," I whispered as loudly as I could, wishing so very much that I could follow him, to be with them both once again.

I turned and began making my way towards my house. Remembering the package I stopped to unwrap the cloth and held the wooden penis up to the moonlight. Being tightly bound in the finest silk it felt wonderfully smooth.

I put the object to my lips and gave its tip a kiss.

"Thank you," I said quietly in the warm night before making my way back to my bedroom.

Amour Noir
by Landon Dixon

I stood in the rain, looking at the sign in the window, 'Man Wanted'.

When I shoved the door of the diner open, I was blown inside by a wet gust of wind. The door sucked closed behind me, and I gave the joint the once-over: red vinyl-cracked stools fronting a white counter, red vinyl booths with white Formica tables along the wall, black and white tiles on the floor. The place was lit too bright and reeked of grease and urinal pucks, completely deserted except for a small, oily character dressed in white perched on a stool next to the cash register, reading a paperback.

A real Sioux City hot spot.

But it was way past midnight, and I was way past hungry. There were still eighty-five miles to go before I reached Sioux Falls and the Tri-State County Managers convention.

'Sure coming down out there,' I said amiably, slipping off my raincoat and tossing it over the back of a booth bench, sliding in opposite.

The little guy squatting by the register lifted a pair of liquid brown eyes and looked at me. His dark, shiny hair was parted down the middle, a brown, unlit cigarette dangling from the corner of his mouth. The nametag on his chest read 'Sinjin'. He blinked his long lashes a couple of times and then bowed his head back down to his book, '*You Play the Black and the Red Comes Up*'.

I plucked a stained menu out of the rack on the table and opened it up, hoping the food was better than the service. Then the service got better - way better.

A red, plastic catsup container rolled across the floor, bumped against my foot. I looked up, and there she stood, in the swinging door to the kitchen – a cool, tanned blonde in a blazing white skirt and blouse, slender arms and legs gleaming bare, honey-blonde hair cut shoulder-length, wavy and glossy. Her eyes were blue, and they sparkled, her high breasts bobbing as she walked my way. The whole package dazzled these sore eyes.

'See anything you like?' she double-entendred, bumping up against my table. The nametag on her chest read 'Chrissie'.

'Weeell,' I said, getting in on the game. 'Matter-of-fact, my appetite's really picked up.'

Her moist lips curved into a smile. 'A hungry

man's good to find,' she cooed, tossing a disdainful look over her shoulder at Sinjin. The guy had his foreign-made coffin nail lit now, was puffing up a storm.

'Food's pretty cheap here, too, eh?' I said, glancing down at the menu. 'I hope it tastes–'

'You won't find anything *cheap* around here!' Chrissie retorted, eyes flashing.

I couldn't come up with any other pithy come-ons, so I ordered the hamburger steak platter and a cherry Coke. It came and went, lying heavy in the pit of my stomach as the blonde dish pushed out her chest and asked, 'Dessert?'

'Something sweet and sticky?' I suggested.

'Pie?' she responded, wagging a smooth, brown leg back and forth, toeing the tile.

'Sure, what kind of *pie* do you have, Chrissie?'

'Cora.'

I looked up her leg, to her chest. 'Cora?'

'That's the ticket, Frank,' she giggled, all sweet and sticky.

I didn't know what kind of a game we were playing now. My name isn't Frank, and hers wasn't Cora. But I let it ride. 'Uh, the kinds of pie?' I reminded her.

She hooked a red-tipped finger into her crimson lower lip, blue eyes twinkling. 'Hmmm, I can't quite seem to remember. They're all in the kitchen – come and see for yourself.'

The place was empty now. Sinjin had skulked off five minutes earlier, the joint going up a full star with his exit. The only sounds were the night rain washing against the steamed-up windows, the wind rushing down the empty ribbon of wet asphalt outside. And the thumping in my chest.

I climbed to my feet.

'Cora' led the way, round hips swishing, mounded buttocks sluicing, lithe legs whispering, through the swinging door and into a cramped, confused kitchen. She halted the parade in front of a flour-strewn counter and turned to face me. Slender fingers brushed across her soft throat, toyed with the top button on her blouse.

'Where's the pie?' I asked, looking around. I do like my pie.

'You're a drifter, aren't you?' Cora breathed. She fluttered her eyelashes, unbuttoned her buttons. 'A stranger in town.'

'Uh, actually, I'm heading for–'

'Don't talk, Frank,' she cut in, pressing a finger to my lips. 'You rang twice, and I'm here. That's all that's important.'

The woman's eyes were elsewhere. And so were mine, because she had her blouse open now, revealing a white, satiny bra that packaged her pair of cupcakes beautifully – up and out. I licked my lips, the babe's sweet perfume flooding my good senses. I didn't understand any of her role-playing rigmarole, and I didn't care.

She ensnared me in her arms, kissing me, her breasts pushing warm and insistent into my chest, soft, wet lips sucking the breath out of me. I grabbed her and hungrily kissed back, grinding my swelling cock into her warm belly. She moaned, running her fingers through my black locks, then clutching at my hair, really digging her hooks into me.

'I wanted you from the moment I saw you, Frank,' she murmured.

She was off in a world of her own, but the reality of her heaving chest was very near and dear to me. I grasped her breasts, squeezing the pert nubbins, forcing groans of pleasure from her lips. Then she popped her bra open at the back and I went skin-on-skin with her bikini-pale tits, kneading the smooth, heated flesh, pinching her pink nipples.

'Suck my breasts, Frank!' she implored.

I bent my head down and flicked a nipple with my tongue, watching in amazement as it instantly grew in size and rigidity. Cora's body quivered in my hands. I lapped at the undersides of her rubbery nipples, swirled my tongue around and around their pebbly aureoles.

Cora squirmed in my arms, then dropped right out of them, down to her knees on the floor. She quickly unbuckled and unzipped me, dragged my swollen cock out of the tangle of my underwear and out into the steamy open. We both watched it grow rock-hard, her hand pulsing its heartbeat.

I flooded with heat, trembling. She smiled up at me, then sent her silky hand sailing up and down the throbbing length of my prick, sending shivers of delight radiating all through me. She stroked and stroked my cock, raw and hot and honest before finally squeezing the pulsating shaft and sticking out her pink tongue and swabbing the tip of my straining dick with the tip of her tongue. I flat-out vibrated with the wet, erotic impact.

Then I smelled smoke. I twisted my head around – there were puffs of white, acrid smoke billowing through the crack in a black curtain that marked off the entrance to some sort of storage room. I'd smelt that smoke before, scared now there was going to be fire.

'What the–'

'That's just my husband,' Cora stated, winding her tongue around the bulbous hood of my cock. 'Sinjin likes to watch.'

I started to say something, started to tuck my hard-on back in and beat a hasty retreat from that greasy loony bin. But before I could finish anything I'd started, Cora inhaled me almost right down to the roots. And all bets were off.

'Jeez!' I groaned, ablaze in the wet-hot cauldron of the woman's mouth. I weaved my fingers into her yellow hair and hung on for the ride.

She eagerly bobbed her pretty head back and forth, velvet lips sliding along my gleaming, vein-popped pole. She sucked and sucked on my cock, pulling hard and long, fingering my tightened ball sack, building and building the pressure, setting me to shaking with sensation.

Just as I was about to blow sky-high, she suddenly pulled back, dropping me dripping out of her glorious mouth.

She jumped to her feet, up onto the counter. And I shoved her back, unthinking, just doing, yanking off her skirt and panties and exposing her dewy blonde need.

'Fuck me, Frank!' she exhorted, crushing her bare breasts in her hands.

I shouldered her legs and recklessly steered my cockhead into her bush, through slick petals and deep into hot, wet, tight pussy. She rolled around in the flour, moaning. I churned my hips as I fucked her.

The counter creaked and the flour flew as I pumped the writhing woman, the smoke from our puffing voyeur hazing the kitchen but not quite muffling the tangy, desperate smell of sweat and sex. I gritted my teeth and flung my hips at Cora, pistoning granite dong into gripping cunt. I was on fire, out-of-control, body and balls tingling way past the point of no return.

'Yeah, Cora, yeah!' I hollered, fucking the blonde in a frenzy.

Then I was jolted by orgasm, my thrusting pipe exploding inside her sucking pussy, filling her with white-hot ecstasy. She screamed her own joy, legs shaking against my chest and body shuddering, fiery orgasm engulfing the both of us.

I stayed longer than my budgeted one hour for dinner in Sioux City.

I soon came to realize why I'd never met anyone like Cora before: most people who thought and acted like she did were locked up somewhere, safely away from square johns like myself. The woman had some serious delusions – about movies. Not girlish crushes on matinee idols like Brad Pitt or Tom Cruise, or displaced dreams of being the next Scarlett Johansson or Catherine Zeta-Jones. No, this offbeat babe had a living, breathing, all-encompassing Film Noir fetish.

She told me all about it, gushing it out with the same intensity she'd gushed earlier. All about the black and white shadowy lighting, the furtive characters and seedy locations, the sexy, sinister themes, the motion pictures and movie actors and studios; an alternative rain and tear-streaked chiaroscuro world of brooding heavies and smouldering femmes fatales, doomed lovers and desperate loners. A strange, exciting, flickering world that was her escape from a shabby Sioux City existence, I supposed.

Sinjin indulged her fantasy role-playing, as she indulged his fisted voyeurism. And now I'd become the third pointy-head in the whole crazy lust triangle. I'd been caught between the nutty dame's legs and she wasn't about to let go.

We hooked-up again the following evening, the setting: an abandoned warehouse overlooking the misty banks of the Missouri River. I was costumed in a flimsy trench coat and a wrinkled fedora, playing the rogue cop, 'Bannion'. Chrissie/Cora was now Debbie, the bad-girl gangster's moll desperate to redeem herself. Sinjin held down his usual supporting role as the peeping, puffing tom in the shadows.

Pipes dripped unknown liquids and tiny feet scurried about, towers of crates creaking ominous warnings, as Debbie set the scene of dangerous love by scrambling out of her little, black moll gown and up onto a pile of coiled ropes. She wagged her bare, tan and white, bottom at me. I moved in behind, gripping the glowing orbs of her bum and sinking my shaft into her pussy. Her desperate cries and my urgent grunts echoed in the gloomy, cavernous confines, Sinjin's cigarettes burning bright orange behind a rusted metal pillar.

The next night, the scene shifted to a dank alley that ran into oblivion alongside a sleazy bar. I was the hardboiled private dick, 'Sam', who plastered soft, willing, manipulating 'Brigid' up against a grimy brick wall and tried to hose some truth out of her. Sinjin was third garbage can on the right, watching and puffing and pulling in the dark.

Night after rainy night it went on and on, through the dog-eared celluloid catalogue of con-men and suckers, vulnerable good girls and brassy broads. It all became way too much for me. I'm a Kung Fu genre fan, myself, and not much of a ham. Not to mention the fact that my boss back home was really wondering why it was taking so long to 'get my car fixed' in Sioux City.

'It's been a lot of, um, fun...'

'Phyllis.'

'Phyllis,' I broke it to the blonde hottie, as she drove us to a seedy downtown hotel through another liquid night. 'But I've got to get back to work. I can't afford to lose my–'

'No one's pulling out!' she sneered, strangling

the steering wheel. 'We went into this together, and we're coming out at the end together. It's straight down the line for both of us.'

We skidded to a stop in front of the glowering hotel and rented Room 1313 from a nebbish desk clerk wearing a leer the size of all Iowa. Phyllis unlocked the door to the ratty room, unloaded a bottle of rye from a paper sack. She filled a pair of dirty water glasses, and drank from both.

'I'm crazy about you, Walter,' she breathed, standing on tip-toes and smothering my mouth, drawing blood with her teeth.

I was the hapless stooge trapped in the erotic clutches of the calculating femme fatale; playing a hopeless game in which I didn't even know the rules or the players.

Phyllis shoved me down to my knees on the threadbare carpet, ordered me to polish the four-inch black stilettos she had strapped to her feet – with my tongue.

I looked up the smirking woman's slim, stockinged legs, up and under the knee-high black skirt she was wearing without the benefit of panties. She gestured impatiently, and I hung my head, licked the rounded tip of her shoe.

A gold anklet encircled her left ankle, glittering in the light. I coiled my trembling fingers around it and lifted her foot, ran my tongue all along the high-polish leather of her shoe, tasting the rich, smooth texture. Then I lapped at her other high heel, licking the shimmering bridge of her foot where it humped out of her shoe.

Phyllis stripped off her pink sweater, baring her breasts. She cupped and fondled her handful tits, rolling engorged nipples between her fingers. She stuck a spike heel in my face and I dutifully snaked my tongue around it, then sucked on it, desperate to please.

When I'd worshipped at her feet long enough, she unhooked her skirt and slid onto the bed. She spread her legs and beckoned, and I crawled across the floor, in between her silken stems. I stuck my tongue into the damp, blonde fur of her pussy without hesitation.

'Yes!' she moaned, clawing at my hair. 'Eat me, Walter!'

I gripped her taut thighs and lapped at her slit, anxiously tonguing her from bum hole to mound-top, over and over. She was wetter than night. Her spicy juices and musky scent made my addled brain spin even faster.

'Enough!' she commanded at last. She gestured at me to stand up, strip off my clothes.

I wiped off my mouth and stood, stripped, shooting a quick glance around the dingy room for that tell-tale smoke. Phyllis pointed at the cracked mirror on the wall, which I took to be of the two-way variety. Then she grabbed me and spread me out on the bed, herself on top.

She grasped my cock and speared it between her slickened lips, sitting down on it. 'Mmmm, that feels good, Walter,' she exhaled, digging her scarlet fingertips into the hair on my chest and moving her bum.

I gripped her hanging tits, tried to meet her urgent bouncing with my own upward thrusting. But I didn't have the strength, or the stamina. Phyllis vigorously shifted her ass up and down, riding my achingly hard cock, fucking me with her pussy.

The sagging bed squealed in agony, the blonde picking the tempo up to frenzy-mode. The headboard cracked against the ragged wallpaper until the whole room shook with the ferocity of her passion. I lay there in a pool of our sweat, body limp, cock surging with sexual electricity.

'Yes, Walter, yes!' Phyllis screamed.

She tore at my chest, bouncing around like a madwoman, until her dewy body spasmed with the wicked orgasm she pulled from my cock. Her joyous shrieking overpowered my breathless whimpering, as I spurted semen inside her in an orgasm long and loose and full of juice, but utterly lacking in feeling.

Then the door burst open. A man stood there, a huge, angry bear of a man. 'I knew you was cheatin' on me!' he roared at Phyllis. 'You're gonna die, asshole!' he roared at me.

Phyllis sunk her fingernails into my flesh, pinning me down.

She slow-rode my cock, eyeing the brute crowding the doorway with total contempt. 'So, you finally caught on, huh, Nick?'

The big man gaped at her, big, hairy hands clenching into big, hard fists.

'Walter, meet my husband, Nick,' Phyllis/Brigid/ Debbie/Cora/Chrissie said to me.

Then kissed me deadly.

I woke up screaming, pushing the black angel away with a superhuman effort. I jumped to my feet, cock and balls flapping on empty. I didn't know for sure what the hell was going on, but I knew one thing: I was being cast for the real-life part of patsy, pushover, and fall guy all rolled into one, the clay pigeon. The big knife was out and the big heat was on; this was the breaking point, the set-up. I was going to be the accused, abandoned, beyond a reasonable doubt.

The man filling the doorframe suddenly started shaking, spluttering, body and soul, his beefy face burning purple.

'Remember your heart condition, dear,' his

wife jeered, with more than a touch of evil. 'Keel over from a coronary, or tear my lover limb-from-limb and go to jail – either way, Sinjin and I get the diner, and each other.'

I shot a look of despair at the born-to-be-bad piece of blonde ice. But it was too late for tears. I barrelled straight into the third man, sending him slamming backwards into the hall clutching his chest.

I raced down the stairs and out into the dark city, the asphalt jungle, between midnight and dawn; the night runner shooting through a nightmare alley and across a street with no name. I scrambled up a grading and by a narrow margin hooked on to the side of a thundering boxcar, swinging inside, railroaded out of town.

A poor sap on the run now, on dangerous ground, in a lonely place. A guy who'd taken a detour into a roadhouse, a dark passage, and was DOA as soon as he'd stepped through the door. Was there ever a shadow of a doubt?

You Might Like It
by Penelope Friday

"Spank me?" She scoffed. "I'd like to see you try!"

"*I'd* like to see me try. That's the point."

There was an assessing look on his face, as his gaze dropped down to her bottom, curving suggestively under a skirt that covered her to mid-thigh. The look of assessment was returned by her, her head tilted to one side, her dark hair sweeping her shoulder.

"And what would I get out of it?"

He smiled.

"Try it; you might like it."

"Uh-uh. Not tempting enough yet. Persuade me more. What are you going to do for me in return?"

He hesitated. No doubt about it, he hesitated. Weighing up his options, she reckoned. Just as she was weighing up her own. Privately, she'd always had the odd fantasy about being smacked, but he didn't know that. He didn't need to know that. This way, she might get to try out two fantasies for the price of one. A bargain indeed!

She moved towards him, entwining her arms around his neck suggestively; pressing kisses against his cheekbone.

"I could suggest something," she whispered.

He was intrigued, she could see. Also, she could not help being wickedly amused by his anxiety. What on earth did he think she was going to ask him to do? Something so scandalous that he wouldn't be able to consider it without blushing?

"Go on then."

His hands had slid around her to fondle her arse, smoothing the silky material against her sensitive skin. She leaned her head on his shoulder and looked up at him.

"Well," she drawled slowly, "why don't we take things a little further? Why don't we ... set the scene a little first?"

"What do you mean?" he asked.

So she told him...

He leaned heavily on the wooden desk, frowning slightly. Miss Fenella Grant had misbehaved too many times recently. She would have to learn that her behaviour was unacceptable. She would have to be punished. He looked around the book-lined study and waited for her to arrive.

She stood on the far side of the wooden door,

smoothing out any possible creases in her tunic. Had she taken things too far? What would he say to her this time? What would he **do** to her? The tap on the door was timid – so light that she wondered whether he would hear her. But he must have been listening, because a stern voice called out in response.

"Come in."

Her fingers slipped on the door knob as she twisted it. Her palms were just the slightest bit sweaty. She rubbed them against her skirt and tried again. This time, the door opened, and she slid in to the room, standing just inside the door, hands clasped nervously in front of her.

"You wanted to see me, sir?"

"Yes. Yes, Fenella, I did. Come in further and shut that door behind you." She pushed the door to, and noticed a large, old-fashioned key in the lock. "Lock the door, and bring me the key."

"But, sir …"

"No!" He cut across her. "I give the orders in here, Fenella, not you. Lock that door immediately."

"Yes, sir."

She twisted the key. It creaked slightly as the lock turned. Pulling it out, she found that it was lighter than she had expected: it looked so heavy and old. She held it in front of her, offering it to him while staying as far from his desk as she possibly could. He took the key from her hand, and placed it in a drawer. Fenella found that she could hardly breathe. It was just him and her in here now. There was no escape for her. She shuffled back a couple of steps, putting a gap between herself and him.

"Stand still, girl."

"Sorry."

He sat upright, and looked her straight in the eyes. His face was grave.

"Miss Grant, I have been hearing bad reports about you from every side. It appears that you have been misbehaving on a grand scale. I would be sorry to think that any of my students could be so disobedient without due cause. What have you to say for yourself?"

Fenella's heart was beating a little faster. He was *good* at this. How did he get to be so good at this? She could feel an answering throb to her heart lower down, between her legs. She hung her head a little.

"I'm sorry, sir. I didn't mean to be bad."

He rose to his feet, majestically.

"Didn't mean it? You come to me with more disgraceful – disgusting – reports than any other student before you, and all you can say is that you didn't mean it? Miss Grant, you will need to have a better explanation than that if you want to escape punishment."

Oh, punishment! She had been waiting for that word, and she felt a jolt in her stomach as he said it. The word lingered on his mouth like a promise. But she had her part to play, and she was enjoying playing it. She threw herself to her knees in front of him.

"Oh, sir. Oh sir, please don't punish me!"

"Have you been bad, Fenella?" he asked gently.

She looked up at him. He had walked around the desk and was leaning against it – right above her.

"Yes," she whispered.

"Very bad?"

"Very bad, sir."

"Then you must be punished, Fenella. Rules must be obeyed – do you understand?"

"Yes."

"Yes …?" He waited.

"Yes, sir," she corrected herself.

"And you will take your punishment like the naughty girl you are?"

"Yes, sir." (Yes, *please,* she thought.)

He bent down to her and put a hand underneath her chin. It was the first time he had touched her, and she shivered at the feel of his touch.

"You need to stand up, then, girl. Stand up and bend over the desk. But first, you will need to remove your panties – you **are** wearing panties, are you not, Miss Grant?"

"Oh, yes, sir."

"Then stand up and take them off."

She obeyed. Her hands slipped under her tunic skirt as she reached and pulled down a pair of skimpy white knickers. She held them in her hand and turned to him.

"What should I do with these, sir?"

"Put them on my desk. There." He pointed. "They will be directly in front of you when you bend over – a reminder, Miss Grant, of your sins. Are we clear about this?"

"Yes, sir."

"Bend over."

She leaned down across the dark wooden desk. It had a smooth surface, almost comforting against her cheek. She knew that with her motion, her tunic had lifted at the back, leaving her pale, tender bottom open to the elements – and to him.

"What are you going to do to me, sir?" she asked.

She felt a hand against her back, pushing her further down against the desk, so that her breasts were rubbing teasingly against its firmness.

"I am going to teach you a lesson, Fenella." His voice was gentler now, almost loving. He stroked the hand down her back, lifting the bottom of her tunic that little bit further when his hand reached it. "You understand that you need to be taught a lesson, don't you?"

"Yes."

"Yes –?"

"Yes, sir," she corrected herself obediently.

"Good. Remember, this is for your own good, Fenella." He permitted the first trace of laughter to appear in his voice. "I don't say that I get no pleasure from this, but – you know you deserve it."

"Oh yes, sir," she breathed.

His hand rubbed gently across her exposed bottom, leaving every nerve-ending tingling.

"You see, you've been a bad, bad girl."

He lifted his hand away and brought it back with a slap.

"Oh!" She couldn't help but exclaim; it was – it was a little painful but, at the same time … she wriggled her arse a little, suggestively, begging for more.

"Keep still, Miss Grant."

The hand lifted and slapped again; lifted and slapped. There was a rhythm to the punishment that had her moaning against the desktop. Lift – slap – lift – slap.

"Sir!"

His hand paused on her bottom, smoothing the contours.

"Fenella?"

Lift – slap – lift – slap.

"Please…!"

"Please, what, Fenella? You know you deserve your punishment."

She arched her neck back, up from the desk, closing her eyes as she did so.

"Yes, yes, but sir…"

"What?"

"Fuck me," she moaned. "Please – please, fuck me. Please, I need you inside me."

The hand lifted and smacked once more.

"Miss Grant, I am ashamed of you. You are a student, I am a teacher. It would be most inappropriate to do what you suggest."

Slap – slap – slap.

"Yes, yes, I know – but please!" she whimpered, rocking back and forth, so that her nipples grew hard against the wood and she was wet, so wet, between her thighs. His fingers delved lower, noting the heat and wetness that she couldn't disguise.

"Oh, Fenella," he said, his voice a caress. "Oh, what a very naughty girl you are." One finger slipped inside her, pressing against her most sensitive places. "This is a punishment, Fenella. And you … you're wet, you're giving, you're *begging* me, are you not, to make love to you?"

"Yes."

"Yes…?"

"Yes, sir!" The words were almost screamed as one finger became two, became three, thrusting in and out of her.

"Tell me what you want, Fenella. Tell me exactly what you want."

The fingers did not stop their movement for a second. He had no mercy.

"Oh, God." Without the slap of his hand on her arse, she could feel it tingling with need. With his fingers inside her, she could hardly think – hardly breathe – for wanting him. "Darling…"

His other hand was on her neck suddenly; his voice a savage whisper in her ear.

"But I am not your darling, am I, Miss Grant? I am your teacher, and I want to hear you beg. I want to hear every word of your *disgraceful* fantasies. I want to hear everything you've ever dreamed of me doing to you."

She wondered if he could make her come just from the sound of his voice. Perhaps she had not been the only one with this particular fantasy in mind. Her voice grew husky.

"Sir, I … I've been such a bad girl." The

fingers thrust hard inside her and she bucked under his pressure. "I have … I have dreamed, I have wanted you to …" Now his palm was on her bottom again, stroking the reddened skin. It was heaven. "I have imagined you doing just this to me, sir; spanking me until I couldn't take any more, until I screamed out for you …"

"Yes …?"

"Until," her voice sank to a low moan, "until I begged you to take me. Until I was so wet, so throbbing that I couldn't live without you inside me. And then you … you …"

"Tell me more."

"You pushed inside me, sir. You fucked me, over and over and over. I came, and came again, and it was your name – your name, sir – on my lips as I cried my desire aloud. Punish me, sir. I shouldn't have thought such things."

"Oh, Fenella, Fenella." He spoke with mild disapproval. "Oh dear. You are such a very bad girl."

The hand had gone from her neck, and she could hear the sound of him unzipping his trousers. It was unbearably exciting.

"Please, sir!" she begged.

"What did you say you wanted?" he demanded softly. She could feel his erection pressing against her. He was so hard. "Did you want me to do this?" He thrust inside her and she moaned against the desk. "Did you?"

"Oh, yes, sir."

"And then," he continued, pushing further inside her, "you wanted me to ..."

He was moving back and forth, gently at first but with ever increasing pressure until she too was thrusting against him, wantonly demanding and receiving pleasure.

"Yes, yes!"

"Yes ..." His voice was lower, but his breathing too was fast now; she could feel that he was on the edge, close to tipping over.

"Yes," she echoed, and opening her eyes saw the sight of her pure white panties, two inches from her face.

It was the last touch. She came, crying out his name, just as she had told him. She felt him climax, too; throbbing inside her in a heavy breathing silence more sensual than any words could have been.

Later, much later, he spoke again, smiling.

"I think I could grow to like your fantasies, Fenella."

"Me too," she said, contentment etched across her body.

"Me too."

Looking for love? Our unique dating sites offer the perfect way to meet someone who shares your fantasies.

www.xcitedating.com

Find someone who'll turn fiction into reality and make your fantasies come true.

www.xcitespanking.com

Spanking is our most popular theme – here's the place to find out why!

www.girlfun-dating.co.uk

Lesbian dating for girls who wanna have fun!

www.ultimatecurves.com

For sexy, curvy girls and the men who love them.

Also available at £2.99

Confessions Volume 3

Some experiences just have to be confessed!

Topless girls with attitude and icecream equals a lot of messy fun for one man who dares to do more than dream ...

A raid on a fetish club does nothing but increase the voltage of the sexual energy coursing through the bad girls ...

In the great outdoors, when you happen across female strangers misbehaving, watching can be far more exciting than joining in ...

The appetites of the wives of powerful men cannot be underestimated, nor can the delights of satisfying their hunger ...

ISBN 9781907016332

For more information and great offers
please visit
www.xcitebooks.com